VOICES

Respectful but Unafraid

A Novel

By

Linda A. Sanchez

Copyright Page

Printed in the United States of America
First Edition
ISBN: 979-8-9986900-0-6
Cover design by Linda A. Sanchez
Published by Legacy & Light Publishing
Victorville, California
www.legacyandlightpublishing.com

Dedication

For Maximus, Keila, and Malia-
Thank you for being my greatest teachers.
You are the reason this story exists.
Through you, I found my voice.
And through you, I learned how to raise yours.

With all my love,
Mom

Epigraph

Silence was my inheritance.
But I chose to pass down something else—
voice, safety, and the freedom to be heard.

Respect and fear are not the same.
I was raised to confuse them.
I raised mine to know the difference.

A mother's voice is the first permission slip a child is
ever handed—
to speak, to feel, to become.
I made sure mine knew they had the right to all three.

And maybe, in these pages, you'll find the permission
to reclaim your own.

Table of Contents

Chapter One: Dresses

The box was heavier than it looked. Old cardboard, taped at the edges, worn soft from time and storage. Leah hadn't opened it in the three years since her mother passed—not because she forgot, but because she didn't want to remember.

It had her mother's handwriting on the side: **"Leah – Childhood."**

She wasn't sure if that label was meant to be sentimental or territorial. Either way, it made her hesitate.

But today, she pulled back the tape.

Inside were yellowed photo albums, crumpled paper doilies, church programs from decades ago, and then—tucked between a manila envelope and a plastic baggie of old barrettes—she saw it. A photo. She knew the dress before she even saw the full picture.

Red velvet. White tights. Her arms hanging stiff at her sides. She was standing in her aunt's living room, next to her cousins, maybe five years old. The photo wasn't bent, but the memory was.

She didn't remember much about that day, but she remembered the story her cousins told her years later—how, as soon as her mother left, they'd change her out of the dress and tights and put her in play clothes. How they let her be a kid. And then, just before her mom came back, they'd dress her up again, like she'd never left the image behind.

She stared at the photo, and for a moment, she saw it all. The stiffness. The silence. The way she never had a say.

She set the photo aside and reached deeper into the box, her fingers brushing over the edge of another frame. A school picture. Kindergarten—maybe first grade. There she was again. Same forced smile. Same dress-and-tights combination. A tiny girl sitting perfectly upright, hands folded in her lap like she'd been warned not to fidget.

And with it came another memory.

She had walked home from school one day with a snag in her tights and a faint grass stain on her dress. She'd fallen during recess, playing tag—just like any normal kid would. She didn't cry when she hit the ground. But she remembered the way her stomach dropped when she looked down at the damage. Because she knew what would happen next.

Her mother had answered the door, looked her up and down, and said nothing. Just narrowed her eyes and turned away. The punishment didn't come with raised hands that time—but with sharp words about carelessness, about embarrassment. That night, Leah had sat on her bed with a washcloth, scrubbing at the stain like it was a sin. Trying to clean not just the dress—but the shame.

She wasn't trying to ruin anything. She was just playing.

But in her mother's house, there wasn't room for *play*—only for *presentation*.

Years later, Leah stood in the doorway of Lila's room.

Her daughter was eight. She had just picked out her clothes for school the next day. Mismatched socks. A baggy hoodie with a cartoon unicorn on it. Purple leggings that had clearly been worn more than once that week.

"I love your style," Leah said with a smile.

Lila beamed, twirling once. "You don't think it looks weird?"

"Nope. I think it looks like *you*."

That night, she tucked Lila into bed and kissed her forehead. Her daughter looked up at her and said, "Thanks for letting me pick."

It seemed like such a small thing. But it wasn't.

Now, sitting in a sea of her mother's boxes, Leah realized that *those* were the moments she fought for. The ones where she chose differently. The ones where her kids never had to earn their voice—they were simply allowed to have one.

She reached for her journal—the leather one she kept tucked in her nightstand—and flipped to a blank page.

She didn't know if she would ever show them these words. But they needed to be written.

Dear Lila,
You once thanked me for letting you pick your own clothes.
What you didn't know is that it wasn't just about socks and sweaters.
It was about a little girl in a red velvet dress and white tights,
A girl who came home from school with grass stains on her knees and fear in her chest.
A girl who scrubbed her clothes because she was scared of her mother's silence.
I didn't always know what I was doing as your mom, but I knew I didn't want you to feel what I felt—
unheard, unseen, uninvited to be yourself.
So I let you pick.
And in doing that, I picked too.
I picked freedom.
I picked you.

Love,
Mom

Chapter Two: What's for Dinner

The house was quieter now. Maya was in her room, earbuds in, humming along to a song Leah didn't recognize. Lila had moved out for college last fall. And Mateo—her firstborn—had been gone the longest, off living his own life, making his own meals.

Leah stood at the stove stirring a pot of arroz con pollo, the familiar smell wrapping around her like a memory. It was the kind of dish she used to make when the kids were little—one-pot, warm, comforting. She hadn't made it in a while.

She reached up into the cabinet for a spice jar, and her hand brushed the edge of an old recipe card, handwritten and worn. It wasn't her mother's handwriting—her mother never let her in the kitchen, let alone passed down recipes—but it brought her back anyway. Not to her childhood, but to the moment it all began.

She was twenty-eight when she got pregnant with Mateo. Married, but still carrying so much of her past inside her—quiet wounds that hadn't yet healed, but couldn't be ignored anymore.

She remembered lying in bed one night, one hand on her belly, whispering to the tiny life inside her.

"I don't know how to do this," she had said. *"But I promise you—I'll do better than what I had."*

It wasn't just a hope. It was a vow. One born out of fear, and faith, and fierce love for a child she hadn't even met yet.

Mateo was strong-willed from the start. Curious. Expressive. And oh, so honest—especially about food.

One night, when he was around seven, Leah had made dinner for the three of them—something quick, maybe pasta with ground turkey. Lila, younger by a year, ate happily. But Mateo pushed his plate away after a few bites.

"I don't like it," he said.

Leah paused, her back to him as she reached for the sink. Her childhood flared in her mind—the memory of saying *I don't like it* and being met with harsh words, a smack to the back of the head, or worse. You didn't complain. You didn't have opinions. You ate what was in front of you or you paid the price.

But she wasn't that mother.

She turned around and said, "Okay."

Mateo blinked, surprised. "I don't have to eat it?"

"Nope," she said. "But I'm not making a whole new meal either. If you don't want it, you can find something else. Just clean up after yourself."

He nodded and got up, grabbed a slice of bread and a banana, and sat back down. Simple as that.

It became the house rule: *I'll cook. If you don't like it, you have options—but I'm not a short-order cook.*

It wasn't about food. It was about voice. It was about respect. It was about giving her children what she had never been given—*the space to feel, speak, and choose.*

In her mother's house, dinner was a performance. A stage for obedience. The table was not a place for connection—it was a place for control.

There were no discussions. No preferences. No opinions. There was only, *"Eat it, or else."* And even silence wasn't safe.

Leah had spent years at that table, shrinking.

Now, she was building a different kind of table.

Back in the kitchen, she ladled the rice and chicken into a bowl for Maya, left it on the counter with a note: "Dinner's ready. Love you."

She leaned on the counter for a moment, letting the smell of cumin and garlic settle over her.

She had gotten so many things wrong as a mom. But that vow she made to Mateo—that prayer she whispered into her growing belly—she had kept it. She had done better. She had *been* better.

She walked to her room and pulled out her journal.

Dear Mateo,
When I was pregnant with you, I made a promise.
I didn't have it all figured out. I didn't even have a plan.
But I knew what I didn't want to pass down.
I knew I didn't want you to be afraid to speak up.
I didn't want you to eat things you hated just to keep the peace.
I didn't want dinner to be a battle. I wanted it to be a table. A safe one.
You were the first person who taught me how to parent with intention.
Thank you for being patient with me. For growing with me.
And for never being afraid to say, "I don't like it."
You helped me become the kind of mom I once prayed I'd be.
And I'm still trying, every day.

Love,
Mom

Chapter Three: Under My Roof

There was a church flyer on the kitchen counter. Maya had brought it home from school—an invitation to a youth night from a friend. Leah smiled as she picked it up. Neon colors, pizza promises, a bold invitation: *Find Your Purpose.*

She placed it aside gently, her thumb brushing the corner.

It had been years since church was a weekly rhythm in their home. These days, Leah's faith was something quieter—steady and personal. But the flyer brought back a memory. Not of herself, but of Lila. Of the day her middle daughter told her she didn't want to go anymore.

Lila had been about fifteen—sharp, observant, tender-hearted, and just starting to ask harder questions. They were in the kitchen, a Sunday morning like any other. Mateo had already moved out. Maya was still little, sitting at the table with a coloring book. Leah was getting breakfast together when Lila said it:

"Mom… I don't want to go to church today."

It wasn't disrespectful. It wasn't dramatic. It was calm, but certain.

Leah turned, caught off guard. "Everything okay?"

"I just… I don't think I believe the way you do. And I feel weird pretending. I don't want to go just to go."

Leah froze for a moment. Not in anger, but in tension—between what she had always believed and the freedom she had promised her children. Her heart started to race, not because of Lila's doubt, but because she remembered what it felt like to *never* be allowed to question.

She exhaled and nodded. "Thank you for telling me."

Lila looked surprised. "You're not mad?"

"No. It's your journey. Just like mine was mine."

Leah had been dragged to church every Sunday growing up. Nice dress, combed hair, sit still, don't speak. The message was always the same: God is watching. Be good. Be quiet. Don't embarrass the family.

She didn't remember learning about grace or love. Just rules and fear.

There was no space to ask questions—only silence or punishment.

She didn't want that for her children. She especially didn't want it for Lila.

Later that week, Leah made tea and asked Lila to sit with her in the living room. The house was calm—Maya already in bed, the TV off, just the two of them.

"I just want to tell you," Leah began, "why I believe."

She told Lila about the nights she cried as a child, afraid and alone. About the comfort she found in prayer, in whispers to a God she hoped was real. About how her faith had become her anchor—not because someone forced it, but because she found it herself.

"You don't have to believe just because I do," Leah said. "But I'm always here if you want to talk about it. Or ask anything. Or even disagree."

Lila's eyes welled with tears. Not because of guilt—but because she felt safe.

That was all Leah had ever wanted.

Back in the kitchen now, Leah folded the church flyer in half and tucked it into a drawer. If Maya wanted to go, she would take her. And if she didn't, that was okay too.

Faith, she had learned, was never meant to be forced.

Dear Lila,
You once told me you didn't want to go to church anymore.
And for a split second, the little girl inside me panicked.
Not because I was angry—but because I remembered what it cost me to question.
But you were never me.
And I was never her.
So I let you speak.
And I listened.
That moment became one of my proudest as your mother.
Because I didn't shut the door.
I kept it open.
And in doing so, I saw you walk your own road—
with honesty, integrity, and curiosity.
That's what I hoped for.
Not blind belief. But authentic searching.
I love you. All of you. Always.

Mom

Chapter Four: The Way She Needed

The backpack was still sitting by the front door, untouched. Leah hadn't moved it since that morning—partly because she didn't want to look at it, and partly because it reminded her of something she already knew deep down:

Her daughter wasn't okay.

Maya was fifteen now, but she had always been her shadow. Ever since the divorce, when Maya was just five, it had been the two of them more often than not. Her older siblings, Mateo and Lila, were close in age and had each other, but Maya had Leah—and Leah had her. Backyard swings, scooters in the front, hours spent pretending they were Elsa and Anna or Link and Zelda, drawing, dancing, and watching movies. Just the two of them.

Maya had always been expressive. Artistic. Funny. Beautifully sensitive. But also different.

Different in the way she learned. Different in how much longer things took to stick. Different in how the world seemed to weigh a little heavier on her chest.

Leah had picked up on it early. Homework was harder. Instructions needed repeating. But her heart? Her heart was massive. She wasn't behind—she just needed a different kind of map.

And so every year, Leah made sure to talk to Maya's teachers. She told them, *"She's not like every student, and that's okay. Just please don't make her feel less than."* Some listened. Some didn't. But thankfully, by fifth grade, one did. That teacher helped Maya get on an IEP, and for the first time, Maya wasn't struggling *alone*.

Then came sixth grade. COVID. Remote learning. Everything upside down.

And strangely… Maya thrived. At home, with her pace, her space, her rhythm. It worked. It wasn't perfect, but it was *better*.

Seventh grade, though? A whole different story.

Leah had watched it happen slowly at first—Maya's resistance to the mornings. The way she'd linger in bed. The hesitation to get dressed. The quiet, tearful moments that told a truth Maya didn't yet have the words for.

At first, Leah chalked it up to normal teenage transition stuff. New campus, new teachers, new schedule. No more one classroom all day—now it was lockers, multiple teachers, multiple rules. And the bus ride. Alone. Lila and Mateo had always had each other. Maya had… no one.

Some mornings went smoothly. Others felt like navigating emotional landmines. But that one morning? That one broke Leah.

They missed the bus. Maya had been crying, saying she didn't feel good. Not in a way that screamed "I'm faking," but in a way that said, *"I'm drowning."*

Leah offered to drive her. They got in the car. Maya cried the whole ride.

Leah asked gentle questions—*Was it a teacher? P.E.? The locker room? The academics?* But Maya didn't have the answers. She only had the ache.

Halfway there, Leah pulled into a parking lot. Parked. Took a deep breath.

She turned to her daughter and said, "We're going home."

Maya looked at her, startled. "Really?"

"Yeah. We'll figure this out. But today? We go home."

Later that week, Leah began researching homeschooling. It wasn't something she had ever done or even imagined doing. But sitting across from her daughter that morning, watching her try to hold herself together, Leah knew one thing for sure:

No grade, test, or classroom was more important than Maya's well-being.

Yes, Maya had just made a few friends. Yes, it was going to be a shift. But even friendship wasn't enough to keep her in an environment where she didn't feel safe in her skin.

So, Leah made the call.

And for the next year and a half, she homeschooled her daughter.

Not just with lessons—but with grace, with compassion, and with deep, steady love.

Dear Maya,
I knew you were different early on.
Not broken. Not behind. Just uniquely, beautifully wired.
I saw it in the way you processed things, in the way your heart worked harder to carry what others shrugged off.
You didn't need to be fixed. You needed to be *understood*.
That morning—when you sat in the car crying, and I turned us around—I hope you know:
That wasn't me giving up.
That was me choosing you.
I chose your peace over my schedule.
I chose your mental health over grades and systems and "what everyone else was doing."
I chose you, Maya.
Because you've always mattered more than the map.
And I'll keep choosing you, every time.

Love,
Mom

Chapter Five: Let Her Be Nine

There was something about birthdays that always made Lila pause.

While other kids counted down the days, planned parties, begged for bigger cakes or fancier decorations, Lila would wake up quiet. Thoughtful. A little hesitant.

Leah noticed it early on—maybe around five or six years old. That soft sadness in Lila's eyes when someone asked how it felt to be a year older. And then it became a pattern.

By six, Lila finally put it into words.

"I don't want to grow up yet, Mom."

Leah had crouched beside her that morning, brushing a stray hair from her daughter's cheek.

"You don't have to," she said gently. "You can be six for as long as you need to be."

It was such a small moment. But for Leah, it became one of her deepest parenting truths.

Growing up didn't need to be rushed.

She had grown up too fast herself. Not in age, but in pressure. Expected to be composed, mature, obedient. Expected to understand things no child should have to. There was no time to linger in childhood—not when fear shaped every corner of her life.

So when Lila told her she wanted to slow down, Leah heard it as sacred.

She protected it like a gift.

Leah started making small choices that supported Lila's pace. She didn't push makeup. Didn't force more "grown-up" clothes. If Lila still wanted to play with dolls at ten, she played. If she wanted to sit and draw or watch animated movies instead of teen shows, Leah sat right next to her.

And when the world hinted that Lila should be more, act older, or fit into a faster mold, Leah gently but firmly stepped in.

"She's right where she needs to be," she'd say.

One birthday in particular stood out.

Lila had just turned eleven. The party had ended, the guests had gone, and the house was finally quiet. They sat on the couch together, wrapping leftover slices of cake.

"Do you still feel like you don't want to grow up?" Leah asked.

Lila nodded slowly. "I just… like being here. With you."

Leah smiled. "Then be here, baby. Be eleven. Be you."

Not every parent would understand. Some might say Leah was too soft, too permissive, too sentimental.

But what they didn't know was this: when you grow up afraid to be yourself, the greatest gift you can give your children is *time*.

Time to unfold. Time to wonder. Time to just be.

Dear Lila,
You used to tell me you didn't want to grow up.
And I want you to know—I heard you.
Not just your words, but your heart.
You didn't need more responsibility or faster
milestones.
You needed space.
You needed time.
You needed to be six.
And I'm so glad you let me protect that for you.
I'll never regret letting you linger in those younger
years.
Because in that slow growing, I watched something
beautiful unfold—
a girl who knew her pace, trusted her instincts, and
became herself in her own time.

Love,
Mom

Chapter Six: It Wasn't Just a Dress

The conversation started off ordinary enough.

Leah was in the kitchen, half-listening as her mother talked on the phone, asking if Maya had worn the dresses she had sent over. Leah answered honestly, casually.
"No, not yet."

There was a pause on the other end. Then a sharp shift in tone.

"Well, why not?"

Leah felt her chest tighten.
For most of her life, when her mother asked questions like this, she would soften the truth or deflect—not because she wanted to lie, but because she was afraid. That fear had lived in her since childhood. Saying the truth often came with consequences, with guilt, with shame. But this time, something in her decided: no more. No more fibbing just to keep the peace. No more silencing herself to avoid discomfort.

"She just hasn't wanted to."

That silence again—heavy, disapproving. Then came the familiar edge in her mother's voice, the one that always carried judgment, even when it was wrapped in concern.

"You should have made her wear it. She needs to learn how to dress properly. I spent money on those clothes. You know, I try to help, and it feels like it doesn't matter."

Disappointment. Frustration. And just beneath it—guilt. Her mother's words were laced with it, as if Leah should feel bad for letting the dresses hang unworn, for not making her daughter more presentable, more proper.

And in that moment, something changed. Leah didn't feel the familiar fear that used to tighten her throat or silence her opinions. She didn't know exactly what it was—but something shifted inside her, and for the first time, she found the courage to speak up.

Leah didn't raise her voice. She didn't cry. But she didn't back down, either. For the first time in her life, she pushed back.

"No, she doesn't. She's fine. She's allowed to have a say in what she wears. And I just want you to know that we appreciate everything you do and all the clothes you buy for the children. Eventually, she will wear them, but I'm not going to put pressure on them or make them feel forced into doing something—or like they're not good enough just because they're not wearing the clothes. It'll happen when it happens. Naturally. Organically."

The silence on the line turned into static.

Her mother exhaled sharply. "Maybe we should talk later."

Leah took a breath and said, "That's probably a good idea."

She hung up the phone.

And then she just stood there.

Her hands were trembling, her heart pounding. She wasn't sure what had just happened—only that something *had*. Something big. Something long overdue.

She called her best friend and replayed the conversation, voice shaky, eyes wide.

"I think I just stood up to my mom."

It wasn't just about the dress. It never was.

It was about every time she was forced to wear one as a child, no matter how uncomfortable she felt. About every tight pair of white tights that dug into her skin, every silent car ride to a family gathering where she was told to smile and behave and sit still and be someone she wasn't.

It was about the rips in her stockings from recess that led to lectures, about the stains on her dress that made her feel like a disappointment.

It was about never having a choice.

And that phone call—that moment—it was the first time she reclaimed one.

Things shifted after that. Maybe her mother saw the boundary. Maybe she felt it. Either way, the rules of their relationship changed.

Leah didn't start picking fights. But she stopped folding.

She stopped explaining herself every time she made a different choice as a mother.

She started parenting with more confidence, more clarity.

And more grace—for herself.

Dear Me,
You didn't yell. You didn't curse. You didn't slam the
phone.
You just said no.
And for you, that was everything.
It was the first brick you pulled from the wall that
kept you small.
It was the first breath you took as your own woman.
And even though your hands trembled, your spirit
held firm.
You didn't defend Maya just to protect her.
You defended her to heal something in yourself.
And you were right to do it.
It wasn't just a dress.
It was the moment your voice came home to you.

Love,
Me

Chapter Seven: The Voice I Gave Them

Leah didn't grow up with a voice.

She grew up with rules. With fear. With silence that said, *don't speak unless spoken to*—and even then, only say what's safe.

She learned early on that honesty could be dangerous, that disagreement could invite punishment, and that vulnerability was a risk, not a right. So she walked on eggshells. She filtered every thought. She learned to read a room before she dared to breathe.

Her childhood had no space for softness. No room for question marks.

Just obedience. And fear.

When she became a mother, Leah carried that history with her. Not as a blueprint, but as a warning.

She didn't want her children to shrink the way she had.

She didn't want them to lie just to stay out of trouble.

She didn't want them to think love was conditional.

So she made a decision—one that would shape every moment of motherhood that followed:

I will raise children who know they have a voice.

That didn't mean there were no boundaries. No expectations. Leah still believed in respect. In structure. In teaching right from wrong.

But respect wasn't the same as fear.

And boundaries weren't the same as control.

She remembered a conversation with Mateo when he was around twelve. He had disagreed with her about something—calmly, directly. And instead of shutting him down, Leah paused.

"You said that really well," she told him. "Even though I don't agree, I'm proud of how you shared your thoughts."

His shoulders relaxed. He nodded. And they kept talking.

Moments like that mattered.

Lila, too, had a strong sense of self. She often voiced her opinions—about clothes, about routines, about what felt right or wrong. Sometimes they clashed, but even when they did, Leah reminded her:

"You can disagree with me and still be respectful. You can be honest, and still be kind."

With Maya, it looked a little different. She was softer, more internal. Sometimes her voice came out through drawings or tears or simple phrases like, "I don't want to."

And Leah listened.

That, too, was a voice.

Leah knew her children would grow up in a world that wouldn't always welcome their truth.

So she made sure that at home, it would always be safe to speak it.

She didn't always get it right. There were times when she got frustrated, when her own fear or stress got the

better of her. But even then, she tried to circle back.
To apologize. To model what vulnerability looked
like from a parent's side.

Because if she could be honest with them, maybe
they'd learn to be honest with themselves.

Giving her children a voice meant more than letting
them speak.

It meant teaching them that their feelings mattered.

That their instincts were valid.

That they didn't have to earn love by being agreeable.

And that respect didn't mean silence—it meant
listening both ways.

Dear Me,
You didn't grow up with a voice.
But you gave one to your children.
And in doing that, you rewrote the story.
You turned fear into safety.
Silence into conversations.
Rules into relationship.

You didn't just break a cycle.
You built something new.

Love,
Still Becoming

Chapter Eight: Letting Go

Leah stood in the doorway of Mateo's old room, now mostly empty. The posters were gone, the desk clear except for a few notebooks left behind. The bed was still made—neatly, as if it were waiting for his return. But Leah knew: something had shifted.

It wasn't just the space that felt different.

It was *her*.

There was a time when all three kids needed her for everything—snacks, rides, homework help, emotional reassurance, bedtime prayers. Now, they were learning how to live without her in the daily moments. And that was the point, wasn't it? That was always the point.

Still, it didn't make it easy.

Letting go doesn't happen all at once. It happens in pieces.

It happened the day Mateo packed up and moved to Oregon after graduating high school. She had helped him load the car, watched him double check everything—and then hugged him tighter than she meant to when he pulled away.

It happened when Lila, though still living at home and in college, began carving out her own space, her own routines, her own independence. Less questions. More quiet confidence.

It happened when Maya, still so young at the time, asked to live with her dad—and Leah, as much as it tugged at her heart, had always known that day would come. Somehow, she felt it when Maya was little: that part of her journey would include her father. And Leah never wanted her to feel guilty for that.

These were the steps. The slow, silent ones. The ones no one warns you about.

There was a night recently when Leah had gone to check on Maya's old room. It was tidy now, quiet. A few drawings still taped to the closet door. A pencil cup still on the shelf. Reminders of the time she was attached to Leah's hip—of swing sets, scooters, Frozen sing-alongs, and summer afternoons in the pool.

Letting go wasn't one moment. It was a thousand small ones.

It wasn't that Leah stopped being a mother. She would always be a mother.

But now, it was less about direction, and more about *presence.*
Less about guiding, and more about *watching them rise.*

There were still times she wanted to step in—when Mateo sounded tired on the phone, when Lila looked overwhelmed with school, when Maya went quiet in her messages. The instinct to fix, to protect, to wrap her arms around them was still there.

But more often now, she just… held space.

Letting go, she realized, wasn't about absence. It was about *trust.*

And it wasn't just about letting go—it was also about learning. Learning that even as her children grew and became the people they were meant to be, she never stopped being their mother. She simply had to shift the way she showed up. The way she guided them. The way she taught them.

They didn't need her less. They just needed her *differently.* And she had to become a different kind of parent for a different season of their lives.

Trusting what she had planted.
Trusting who they were becoming.
Trusting herself enough to loosen her grip.

Dear Me,
They don't need you the same way anymore.
And that's not failure.
That's growth.

They still need your love.
But now they need it quieter, steadier, without strings.

You are allowed to grieve what's changing.
But don't forget to celebrate what's growing.

Letting go isn't losing them.
It's honoring who they're becoming.

And it's rediscovering who *you* are too.

Love,
Still Mom

Chapter Nine: The Apologies I Owed Myself

There were things Leah never heard growing up.

Not because she didn't need them—but because the people who should have said them didn't know how.

And for a long time, she thought maybe it didn't matter. That you just grow up, move on, bury the hurt, and keep going.

But healing, she had learned, doesn't come from pretending something didn't happen. It comes from acknowledging it. Naming it. And sometimes… offering yourself the very thing you were denied.

So one day—quietly, without ceremony—Leah sat down and wrote the words she needed most.

Not to her mother.
Not to her father.
Not even to her past.
But to *herself.*

I'm sorry you didn't feel safe.
You were just a little girl, and your heart beat fast not from joy, but from fear.
You walked on eggshells, watched every word, every movement.
You were afraid to say, *"I don't like this."*
Afraid to say, *"That hurt."*
Afraid to just… be.

I'm sorry for every time you had to smile when you wanted to cry.
I'm sorry no one noticed the way your eyes changed when you were scared.
I'm sorry they called it "being dramatic" instead of seeing it as pain.

I'm sorry you didn't get to play freely.
That dresses and tights were more important than joy.
That grass stains were treated like moral failures.
That appearances were everything, and expression was nothing.

You were never meant to be a mannequin.
You were a child.
And I'm sorry they didn't let you live like one.

I'm sorry you had to earn love.
That affection was conditional.
That approval was currency.
That "good girl" meant *"quiet, small, obedient."*

You didn't need to earn love.
You were already worthy of it.

And I'm sorry you thought it was your fault.
The yelling.
The silence.
The shame you carried into adulthood.

It wasn't your fault.
It was never your fault.

Leah didn't cry when she wrote those words.
Not right away.

But later that night, lying in bed, she felt a quiet
loosening in her chest.
Like a knot had finally given way.
Like something buried had finally been seen.

She didn't need anyone else to say it.
Not anymore.

She had said it for herself.

And sometimes, that's where real healing begins.

Dear Me,
You didn't get the love you needed in the way you needed it.
But you gave it anyway—to your children, to your home, to yourself.
You chose softness over silence.
Presence over performance.
Grace over guilt.

And now, you get to be free.

Love,
The woman you became

Chapter Ten: When They Teach You

People always talk about what you teach your children.

They don't talk enough about what your children teach *you*.

Leah went into motherhood thinking she would be the one shaping them—guiding, protecting, molding. And she did.

But what she didn't expect was how much *they* would shape *her*.

Not through lectures or life-altering conversations, but through moments. Small, surprising, sometimes challenging moments that turned into mirrors. That reflected her gaps. Her growth. Her grace.

Mateo taught her how to lead with patience.

He was her firstborn—the one who made her a mom.

She remembers fumbling through those early years, afraid of making mistakes, worried about doing it "right." But Mateo never asked her to be perfect. He just needed her to be present.

There were times he challenged her, pushed boundaries, made her question her instincts. But what she remembers most was the way he watched her—closely, quietly.

He taught her that leadership doesn't always look like control.

Sometimes, it looks like slowing down.

Sometimes, it looks like listening first.

Lila taught her how to honor individuality.

Lila was expressive from the start—creative, emotional, full of opinions and questions. She didn't follow every path set before her. She carved her own.

Leah had to learn not to take it personally when Lila didn't want to do something her way.

She had to resist the urge to correct or redirect, and instead learn to support.

Lila taught her that love isn't about shaping someone into who *you* think they should be. It's about seeing who they *already are*—and cheering them on as they grow into it.

Maya taught her how to slow down and see.

Maya was different—softer, more sensitive. She didn't always speak her feelings out loud. But Leah learned to listen in other ways.

In the way Maya hesitated before answering a question.

In the way her shoulders tensed when something felt too big.

In the way she lit up when she felt understood.

Maya reminded Leah that every child needs something different—and that parenting isn't a formula. It's a relationship.

She also taught Leah that protecting your peace sometimes means *letting go of the plan.*

There were times Leah felt like she was the one teaching—discipline, responsibility, manners, courage.

But more often than not, her children were teaching her how to show up with honesty, humility, and grace.

Dear Mateo, Lila, and Maya,
You made me a teacher.
But you also made me a student.

You taught me that growth doesn't stop with age.
That being a parent doesn't mean having all the
answers.
That love is a daily practice—not a lesson to be
mastered.

Thank you for being my greatest teachers.
Thank you for growing with me.

Love always,
Mom

Chapter Eleven: If I Could Tell My Mother Now…

There are things I never got to say to you.

Some because I didn't have the words.
Some because I was too afraid to speak them.
And some because I knew—even if I said them—you might not hear them.

But if I could tell you now, this is what I'd say:

You were not all bad.

You provided for me. You cooked. You kept things clean.
You made sure I was dressed and fed.
You did what you thought was right, what you believed was best.
I don't doubt that you loved me… in the way you knew how.

But love without safety is a confusing thing.

And your love often came laced with fear.

Fear of saying the wrong thing.
Fear of not looking the way you wanted.
Fear of falling short in ways I didn't understand.

I wish you had known that you didn't have to be
perfect to be kind.
That you didn't have to be strong to be soft.
That being a mother didn't mean controlling—it
meant seeing.

If I could tell you now…

I'd say I forgive you.
Not because what happened didn't matter.
But because I matter more.

I forgive you so that I can move forward.
So I don't pass on what was passed down.
So my children never have to unlearn the things I had
to.

I would tell you that I stood up to you once.

It was just a phone call—nothing explosive.
But it was the first time I found my voice.
And it changed me.

I wonder if you noticed.

I think you did.

Because things shifted after that.

You softened. Just a little.
Maybe not with words, but in energy.

And for that, I'm grateful.

If I could tell you now…

I'd say thank you.
Because even though it was hard—
Even though I had to rebuild so many pieces of
myself—
You gave me the blueprint for what *not* to repeat.

You made me intentional.

You made me protective.

You made me strong in the quietest, fiercest ways.

If I could tell you now…

I'd say I hope you've found peace.
And that somehow, in your own way, you know I
have too.

Dear Mom,
We may never have had the conversations I longed
for.
We may never have hugged with ease or talked
without tension.

But I did love you.
And I always will.

And if you could see me now—really see me—
I think maybe you'd be proud.

Love,
Your daughter

Chapter Twelve: Their Own Voice

Leah used to wonder if she was doing enough.

Enough to protect them.
Enough to prepare them.
Enough to raise them into people who could stand on their own—and stand tall.

She knew what it was like to grow up without a voice. And because of that, she raised her children differently. Intentionally. Gently. Honestly. She gave them space to explore, express, question, and speak up.

And now, slowly, she was beginning to see it—not in grand declarations or dramatic speeches, but in the small, steady ways her children used their voice.

Mateo had always been observant—quiet but thoughtful.
After moving to Oregon, he called Leah one evening and told her he had turned down a job offer.

"It paid well," he admitted, "but it didn't feel right."

Leah asked him why.

"Because they wanted someone who'd just follow every rule without speaking up. And I can't do that."

She smiled. He didn't say it to impress her. He said it like it was obvious. Like *of course* he couldn't stay silent in a space that didn't feel right.

That was voice.
That was values.

Lila had her own kind of voice—creative, passionate, direct.
In her college writing class, she wrote an essay about childhood identity, and how society tries to put girls in boxes. She emailed Leah the draft one night.

Leah read it, tears gathering in her eyes.

"You never made me feel like I had to be anything I wasn't," Lila had written. "And that gave me the freedom to figure out who I was."

Lila wasn't afraid to speak her truth.
And she wasn't afraid to share where it came from, either.

Maya's voice was quieter, but no less powerful. When she moved in with her dad around age twelve, Leah felt a deep ache—but also a strange peace. She had known this day might come.

Years later, Maya sat next to Leah during a weekend visit and said, "Thank you for never making me feel bad about choosing to live with him."

It was such a simple statement. But it held a lifetime of understanding.

"You always gave me room to figure out what I needed," she added.

That, too, was voice—not just speaking, but naming your needs. Not just expressing, but trusting someone would listen.

Watching them now, Leah realized she didn't just raise children who could speak.

She raised people who knew *when* to speak.
How to speak.
And what they stood for when they did.

Dear Me,
You did it.

You didn't just break the silence—you taught them not to fear their own sound.

They speak with kindness.
They speak with courage.
They speak with clarity.

And because of that… so do you.

Love,
Still Listening

Chapter Thirteen: The Things I Kept

Leah sat cross-legged in the garage, surrounded by boxes.

Some were labeled in her own handwriting—**Lila's Art, Maya – Kindergarten, Mateo's Drawings**—and others were older, their corners worn, the ink faded.

Some belonged to her mother.

She hadn't gone through them in a while. After her mother passed, Leah had brought them home, unsure of what to do with the remnants of a life that had shaped her so deeply—both in love and in pain.

She had kept them because… well, that's what you do.
You keep things, even when you don't know why.
You hold on—sometimes out of grief, sometimes out of guilt, and sometimes… just because it's too hard to let go.

But today felt different.

Today felt like a day for remembering. For choosing.

She opened the first box slowly. Inside were old photographs, yellowed with time. Her mother as a young woman. Leah as a child—hair pinned back, eyes wide, wearing another dress she didn't pick out.

She placed it aside.

Underneath it, a folded piece of paper—an old school report card. "Talks too little in class." Leah smiled softly. If only they knew why.

She placed that aside too.

But in another box, she found something else.

A note Lila had written her at age ten: *Thank you for listening to me.*
A drawing from Maya—a picture of a heart with two stick figures holding hands.
A crumpled napkin with a scribbled message from Mateo: *Mom, I'm glad you're mine.*

These she didn't set aside.

These she kept.

It wasn't just the objects.
It was what they represented.

She kept the courage it took to stand up to her mother.
She kept the softness she had to fight for.
She kept the lessons her kids taught her.
She kept the warmth she built in her home.
She kept the voice she had finally claimed.

She let go of the shame.
She let go of the silence.
She let go of the pressure to be perfect.

There were things her mother passed down without
meaning to.

But Leah had learned: just because something is
handed to you doesn't mean you have to carry it
forever.

You get to choose what stays.
And what doesn't.

Dear Me,
You kept what mattered.
You honored the past, but you didn't live in it.
You learned to tell the difference between a wound
and a legacy.
And you chose to pass down love instead of fear.
Voice instead of silence.
Grace instead of guilt.

That's what real inheritance looks like.

Love,
Still Choosing

Chapter Fourteen: Roots and Wings

It was something Leah had come to understand only with time.

When her children were small, they clung to her. For answers. For safety. For comfort. Her lap was their home base. Her voice, their calm. Her presence, everything.

But with each passing year, she watched them stretch further and further beyond her reach—first a few feet, then a few miles, then whole cities away.

She used to fear that distance.
Now, she saw it differently.

Giving them roots had meant giving them a place to return to.
A foundation built on presence, not perfection.
A home where they knew they were loved—on their best days, and their worst.

She gave them history.
She gave them warmth.
She gave them permission to ask hard questions and still be held close.

And she gave them a mother who kept showing up.

But she also gave them wings.

She let Mateo go to Oregon, even when part of her
wanted to hold him back.
She let Lila question things—even when it challenged
what Leah believed.
She let Maya move in with her dad—without guilt,
without fear, without punishing her for needing
something different.

She let them become.

Even when it was hard.
Even when it hurt.

Because love wasn't control.
It was release.

She realized now that parenting had always been both.

Roots and wings.
Safety and freedom.
Presence and letting go.

Dear Me,
You anchored them in love.
You watered them with truth.
You sheltered them with grace.
And when the time came, you opened the gate and
watched them soar.

You didn't lose them.
You lifted them.

Love,
Still Growing

Chapter Fifteen: Full Circle

The house felt alive again.

Not in a loud, chaotic way—but in the way that only happened when all three of them were home at the same time. Mateo was stretched out on the couch, flipping through a photo album with a familiar smirk. Lila sat cross-legged on the rug, a bowl of popcorn in her lap, scrolling through old family videos on the TV. And Maya had taken over the recliner, curled up with a blanket, giggling every few minutes at something one of her siblings said.

Leah sat on the floor beside them, her legs tucked under her like she used to when they were toddlers and she read bedtime stories.

It was her idea. A quiet afternoon together. Just the four of them.

She had pulled out the bins from the hallway closet—photos, DVDs, handwritten notes from Mother's Day, baby clothes she couldn't let go of. There was no special occasion, no holiday. Just a feeling. A pull.

On the screen, a grainy video played: Mateo at five, wearing a superhero cape, jumping off the patio step.

He turned toward the camera with a toothy grin and shouted, "Did you see that, Mom?!"

Leah laughed softly, the memory washing over her.

"You always wanted to fly," she said.

Mateo grinned. "Still do."

Another clip: Lila, maybe six, wearing a princess dress over pajama pants, standing on a stool in the kitchen, helping Leah stir pancake batter.

"Oh my God," Lila groaned, hiding her face, "Why did I dress like that?"

"Because you had style," Leah said, nudging her. "And because I let you."

Lila smiled. "Yeah… thanks for that, by the way."

Then Maya appeared on screen—chubby cheeks, swinging on the backyard playset, belting out a song from *Frozen* at the top of her lungs.

Maya groaned. "Mom, why did you record *everything*?"

"Because you were magic," Leah said without hesitation.

Maya didn't reply, but her smile said everything.

They watched and laughed and paused and rewound. Sometimes they cried. Sometimes they sat in silence, letting a single image carry its own weight.

"Remember that summer?" Lila asked.

"When I burned the burgers?" Leah offered.

"When we all slept in the living room because the A/C broke."

"Oh, right!" Mateo laughed. "We looked like sardines."

"And you two kept stealing the blankets," Maya added, pointing at her siblings.

They talked for hours. No phones. No distractions. Just time.

At one point, Leah looked around and tried to capture the moment in her mind. Grown children, adult voices, the wisdom in their eyes. And yet, beneath it all—*still hers.*

She hadn't done everything perfectly. But she had loved them with everything she had.

She had broken cycles.

She had made new choices.

She had planted gentleness where once there was fear.

And somehow, in all the mess and mystery of motherhood, they had grown into people she admired—kind, honest, funny, thoughtful. Each different. Each whole.

Dear Mateo, Lila, and Maya,
I didn't know what I was doing when I started this journey.
I just knew I didn't want to repeat what was done to me.
So I loved you the best I could.
Sometimes afraid. Sometimes unsure.
But always, always with everything I had.

And sitting here with you—watching you laugh, watching you remember—
it feels like maybe I did okay.

Thank you for being the reasons I grew.
Thank you for loving me even when I was still learning how to love myself.

You're my full circle.

Love always,
Mom

Chapter Sixteen: Becoming Me

The house was quieter now.

No backpacks by the door.
No early morning alarms.
No sibling squabbles over who got the last of the
cereal.

There were still signs of life—framed photos, books
left on the coffee table, music humming from another
room. But the rhythm had changed. Slowed.

Leah stood in the hallway one afternoon, holding a
sweater that belonged to Lila, left behind from her last
visit. She smiled. Folded it neatly. And placed it on
the shelf.

So much of her life had been built around *them*.
Schedules. Meals. Routines.
Emotions. Lessons. Laughter.

But now, in this quiet space between what was and
what was next, she felt something new rising inside
her.

A question.

Who am I now that they're grown?

She had always been a mother.
A protector.
A listener.
A space maker.
A voice giver.

But now, she was rediscovering the pieces of herself
that had been waiting patiently in the background.

She was a woman who loved long walks in the late
afternoon sun.
Who had favorite songs and books and memories no
one else knew.
Who was still curious. Still growing. Still unfolding.

She didn't feel lost.

She felt… open.

Because motherhood had never been her only identity.
It had been a powerful part of her, yes. But not the
whole of her.

She was still Leah.

Still thoughtful. Still creative. Still full of a million
little stories that weren't just tied to her children—but
to *herself*.

She had done the work.
She had raised them well.
She had let go and loved them through every stage.

And now, she was giving herself permission to keep
becoming.

Dear Me,
You were never meant to disappear in motherhood.
You were meant to expand.
And now, in this quiet space, you've found yourself
again.

Not as someone new.
But as someone finally seen.

You are not just who you raised.
You are who you've become.

Love,
Becoming You

Epilogue

I used to think breaking the cycle would look like a fight.
But it looked more like a conversation.
A listening. A pause. A hug in the hallway. A moment where I said, "It's okay. You don't have to be ready yet."

It looked like my children teaching me as much as I taught them.
It looked like grace showing up quietly and often.

And maybe that's the real legacy—
Not perfection. Not control.
But presence.
Voice.
And love, passed on gently, again and again.

Author's Note

This story was born from a very real place in my
heart.

While the characters in this book are fictional, the
emotions behind them are not. The journey of Leah—
and her children, Mateo, Lila, and Maya—was shaped
by pieces of my own motherhood, my own healing,
and the intentional choices I made to raise my
children differently than I was raised.

I grew up without a voice. I walked through childhood
on eggshells, unsure if I could speak, feel, or even
choose freely. And when I became a mother, I knew I
wanted more for my children. I didn't want them to
grow up afraid to speak or to shrink themselves to fit
someone else's comfort. I wanted them to feel safe,
seen, and heard—not only as my children, but as
people becoming.

The themes in this book—*voice, freedom, self-
discovery, and unconditional love*—reflect the
heartbeat of what I tried to build in my home. It hasn't
always been perfect, but it's been intentional. And
that intention has changed everything.

If you've ever felt silenced, unseen, or unsure of how
to parent differently than you were parented, I hope
this story reminds you that it's possible. That healing

is possible. That giving your children a voice doesn't
mean giving up your own—it means finding it
together.

Thank you for reading.
Thank you for holding these pages with tenderness.

With love and hope,

Linda A. Sanchez

Your Voice Matters: A Reflection Guide for Parents

This story began with one mother's journey — but it's meant for anyone who has ever tried to break a cycle, raise children with intention, or love more deeply than they were shown.

Whether you're a mother, father, grandparent, guardian, or someone who helps shape young lives, these questions are for you. May they help you pause, reflect, and rediscover your own voice along the way.

1. What chapter or moment in the book resonated most deeply with you? Why?

2. Did Leah's journey mirror any part of your own parenting story or the way you were raised?

3. Have you ever felt silenced, unseen, or small? How did that affect the way you parent or relate to others?

4. Which of Leah's children — Mateo, Lila, or Maya — did you connect with most? What part of their story moved you?

5. What did your parents (or caretakers) teach you about love, voice, and boundaries? What are you choosing to keep — and what are you choosing to rewrite?

6. What promises have you made to yourself as a parent? Are you living them? What would you change or recommit to today?

7. If you could write a letter to your younger self as a parent... what would it say?

8. If you could speak honestly to your own parent(s), what would you want them to know?

✦ ✦ ✦

 There are no right or wrong answers — only space for honesty, healing, and growth.

About the Author

Linda A. Sanchez is a storyteller, a cycle-breaker, and a proud mother of three. She writes from a deeply personal place — not to preach or pretend to have it all figured out, but to share the journey of trying, learning, healing, and doing better one choice at a time.

She grew up without a voice, but found her own through writing — and made it her mission to raise her children with the freedom and safety she never had. Her memoir, *Lost & Found: The Journey of Socorro*, traces her real-life story of adoption, abandonment, and healing. Her debut novel, *Elena's Quiet Revival*, follows a fictional woman rediscovering faith after silence. *Voices* is her most intimate fictional work yet — rooted in the kind of parenthood that chooses connection over control, grace over guilt, and love that doesn't demand perfection.

Linda is the founder of *Legacy & Light Publishing*, a company created to help others tell stories that deserve to be heard. She lives in the High Desert of California, where she finds joy in slow mornings with coffee and sunlight, deep laughter, spontaneous travel, and time with her husband and children whenever she can. She's a lover of books, life, and the moments that make you feel something real.

To learn more or connect, visit:
www.legacyandlightpublishing.com

Because every story deserves to shine.